WHAT'S THE MATTER, MARLO?

Andrew Arnold

Roaring Brook Press
New York

Marlo is my best friend.
We do everything together.

We read together.

We laugh together.

We play games together.

MARLO!

Our favorite game is hide-and-seek.

Marlo is pretty good
at hiding,

but in the end . . .

. . . I always find him.

When I do, we play something else.

Because we're best friends,
and that's what best friends do.

But not today.
Today, something was wrong.

When I asked Marlo what he wanted
to play, he didn't answer.

Instead, he turned his head, took a
deep breath, and replied . . .

It was clear to me that something was wrong,
so I did what any good friend would do . . . I told a joke.

But that only made
things worse.

Marlo got angrier.

And angrier.

AHHHHHHH

Pretty soon, his anger was
out of control.

At first I didn't know what to do.
But that's when I remembered . . .

. . . I could *always*
find Marlo.

So I looked,

And I looked,

And I looked some more,

. . . eventually,

When I did, I realized that Marlo wasn't just mad,
he was sad, too.

"I'm sorry, Marlo," I said.

And that's when Marlo
and I cried together.

Because we're best friends,
and that's what best friends do, too.

For Beth

In memory of Dakota, Hannah, Gretal,
Gypsy, Trixie, and Chipper

Copyright © 2020 by Andrew Arnold

Published by Roaring Brook Press
Roaring Brook Press is a division of Holtzbrinck Publishing Holdings Limited Partnership
120 Broadway, New York, NY 10271
mackids.com

Library of Congress Control Number: 2019948813

ISBN: 978-1-250-22323-4

Our books may be purchased in bulk for promotional, educational, or business use.
Please contact your local bookseller or the Macmillan Corporate and Premium Sales Department
at (800) 221-7945 ext. 5442 or by email at MacmillanSpecialMarkets@macmillan.com.

First edition, 2020
Printed in China by RR Donnelley Asia Printing Solutions Ltd.,
Dongguan City, Guangdong Province

1   3   5   7   9   10   8   6   4   2